ALICE AND HER MAD HATTERS

A BISEXUAL REVERSE HAREM ROMANCE, ALICE IN WONDERLAND, PORTAL FANTASY ROMANCE

FAE RINGS

BOOK ONE

JAX WILDER

Published by Rainbow Quartz Publishing

RQPublishing.com

RainbowQuartzPublishing@gmail.com

Edmonds, WA 98026

ISBN: 978-1-961714-61-8

Cover design by Miranda Townsend

Edited by Miranda Townsend

First Edition: 2024

For Brandie

Jax Wilder

CHAPTER ONE

Coral Cove always felt a little... off. The kind of off that made people stop mid-step to catch their breath. he way the air hummed with a magic no one could ever quite name, how the sea breeze carried more than just salt and water but a whisper of something deeper. I felt it every time I wandered past the old shops, the odd charm of the place pulling at me, but nowhere as strongly as at *Lilly Drake*.

The chime of bells overhead greeted me as I stepped inside the shop, and immediately, I felt the familiar shift. It wasn't just a jewelry store—it was an escape. A place where the world outside didn't matter.

Lilly Drake wasn't like other jewelry shops. There were no harsh displays of diamond rings or polished gold necklaces. Instead, fairy houses perched in the branches of miniature trees, delicate bridges connecting one whimsical nook to the next. Glass figures hung from the branches, catching the sunlight that filtered in through stained-glass windows, throwing rainbows across the room. The jewelry cases themselves were carved into the "forest," artfully nestled between moss-covered stones and twinkling crystals.

No, this wasn't an ordinary jewelry shop. It was something more, something alive.

"Ah, Alice. I knew you'd come in today." Rainbow Rivers' voice was soft and musical, like wind chimes on a spring afternoon. I turned to see Rainbow Rivers, gliding toward me like she was made of air. Her lavender hair caught the light, her eyes twinkling in a way that told me she knew things I didn't. Her eyes shimmered with a knowing smile, the kind that suggested she understood more than she ever let on.

I smiled, half-shrugging as I looked around. "I don't know why I love this place so much. It's... different. Magical. It just... calls to me."

Rainbow chuckled, her one of a kind hand made sparkling fairy wings fluttering ever so slightly. "That's because *Lilly Drake* holds pieces of magic. Not everyone can see it, but you—" She looked me up and down, as if assessing my very soul. "You always feel it."

My hand drifted over one of the small branches, brushing my fingers across a necklace made of silver and opal stones. "I wouldn't say magic exactly," I replied, though I couldn't quite explain what it was either. "But it's like stepping into another world every time I walk through that door."

Rainbow arched an eyebrow. "And that's why you're here, isn't it?" she asked, that knowing smile still playing on her lips. "You want to escape."

I paused, my fingers tracing the cool surface of a silver pendent. I couldn't lie to her. "Yeah. Lately, it's all I want. I've been feeling... trapped. Like I'm just waiting for something to sweep me away, to take me out of this ordinary life and into something... more."

Rainbow hummed, disappearing behind one of the large trees. "So, you're looking for a little fantasy?"

"Exactly. I mean, who doesn't want to get lost in a good fantasy? Sometimes all I want is to curl up with one of those spicy novels from *Spellbound Stories* and just... disappear into the pages."

Rainbow reappeared, holding a small wooden box in her hands, her expression suddenly more serious. "What if I told you there was a way to disappear into something better than a book?"

I blinked, curiosity tugging at me. "What are you talking about?"

Without a word, she opened the box. Inside was a ring—a simple band of silver with a stone that shimmered like the sky at twilight, casting a thousand tiny rainbows across the shop.

The moment I saw it, I felt it. A hum in the air, like the ring was alive and waiting for me.

"It's beautiful," I breathed, my fingers itching to reach for it. "Can I try it on?"

Rainbow's lips curved into a sly smile, but she shook her head. "No. Not yet."

I frowned, confused. "What if it doesn't fit?"

"It will," she said, her voice confident. "They always do."

Something about the way she said it, like she knew a secret I didn't, made me pause. But I couldn't shake the pull of that ring, the way it seemed to call to me. I swallowed hard. "Okay. I'll take it."

Rainbow's expression softened, but there was a seriousness in her eyes now. She closed the box and held it out to me, her hand lingering on mine just a moment too long. "Before you go... a word of caution. Don't wear it unless you're absolutely sure. The ring knows where you belong. But if they aren't ready to let you come back..."

My heart skipped a beat. "They?"

Her eyes sparkled with something mischievous, something dangerous. "You'll see." She winked and turned away before I could press her for more.

I stood there for a moment, gripping the box in my hand, feeling the weight of her words settling over me like a thick fog. I had no idea what she meant by *they*, but something told me I wasn't going to get an answer.

With a soft thank you, I left *Lilly Drake* and stepped back into the sunlit streets of Coral Cove. The air felt warmer, thicker somehow, as I made my way to the park. The ring still sat in its little box, nestled safely in my bag, but I could feel it, like it was tugging at me, urging me to open it.

I reached the park and slowed my steps. The familiar sight of the swings greeted me, and I couldn't resist. I sat down on one of the old wooden seats, the chains creaking softly as I swung gently back and forth. My fingers found the box in my bag, pulling it out and holding it in my lap.

Rainbow's warning echoed. *Don't wear it unless you're sure.*

I opened the box, staring down at the ring. It glimmered in the fading sunlight, casting tiny rainbows across my skin. My heart thudded in my chest as I reached for it, my fingers trembling slightly.

What's the harm in trying it on?

With one last glance around the empty park, I slipped the ring onto my finger.

The world... shifted.

Everything around me shimmered, the colors vibrating, twisting. My breath caught in my throat as the park dissolved, the swing beneath me vanishing like smoke in the air.

I blinked, my heart racing as the world came back into focus.

I wasn't in the park anymore.

I was somewhere else. Somewhere... impossible.

CHAPTER TWO

I blinked, trying to shake off the haze that clung to me like fog. One second, I'd been sitting on a swing in Coral Cove, and now... what the hell?

The walls around me were mustard yellow and teal, corridors stretching in every direction like some kind of twisted maze. Everything looked like it had been decorated by someone with a grudge against color coordination. I turned in a slow circle, trying to make sense of this strange, claustrophobic place.

Where was I?

I took a few steps down one of the hallways, the silence so thick it felt like I was wrapped in it. "Hello?" My voice echoed back at me, bouncing off the walls.

No answer.

Great. This was just great. I had no idea where I was, no idea how I'd gotten here, and to top it all off, I was pretty sure I'd just seen a rabbit. A white rabbit.

It darted down a hallway to my left, disappearing around a corner. "Oh no, you don't." I muttered under my breath, more out of sheer stubbornness than anything else. If I was stuck in this place, I wasn't going to do it alone. Rabbit or not.

I hurried after it, turning the corner into another long corridor lined with doors. Each one was different—some big, some small, some carved with intricate designs. I stopped in front of a glass table in the middle of the hallway, the only thing that seemed remotely normal.

Sitting on the table was a small key and—was that a bottle? I picked up the key, examining it. It was tiny, barely bigger than my pinkie, and shaped like something from an old-timey fairytale. But it didn't fit any of the doors I'd tried so far.

I glanced at the bottle next. It was small, purple, and a little smoky, like one of those potions you'd see in a witch's shop. Of course, it had a label.

Drink Me.

I rolled my eyes. "Oh, of course. Because that's not suspicious at all."

I paused, feeling the dryness in my throat. I was

thirsty. And assuming I wasn't tripping on some-thing, what was the worst that could happen? Maybe this was all a dream, and I'd wake up soon, safe and sound in Coral Cove.

"Alright, Alice. What's the worst that could happen?" I muttered, popping the cork off the bottle. It smelled oddly sweet, like berries and something floral. Without thinking too much about it, I tipped the bottle back and took a gulp.

For a second, nothing happened.

Then, the world around me started to shift. I stumbled, grabbing the edge of the table as my body... shrank.

"What the—?" I gasped as the table grew taller, the floor rushing up to meet me. The hallways loomed above like a skyscraper, everything growing impossibly big, or maybe it was just me getting impossibly small. My heart pounded as I watched my hands shrink, the key in my palm suddenly feeling like a sword.

I blinked, trying to make sense of the rapid change. "This is... not ideal."

When the shrinking finally stopped, I was standing in a pile of fabric—my clothes. Of course, they hadn't shrunk with me. I looked down at myself, completely naked sans the ring on my finger and now smaller than a Barbie doll.

"Fantastic," I muttered, shaking my head. "At least I'm not cold."

My eyes fell on the key still clutched in my hand. It was big, almost as tall as I was now. An idea sparked, and I grabbed the edge of my discarded shirt, using the sharp corner of the key to slice through the fabric. In a matter of minutes, I had a makeshift dress—if you could call it that. It wasn't pretty, but it did the job.

I looked down at my handiwork and gave a half-hearted shrug. "Could be worse."

Once I'd dressed myself, I took stock of my surroundings again. The doors were even taller now, towering above me like the gates of some ancient fortress. My eyes scanned the room, and I spotted one door I hadn't noticed before. Smaller than the rest, tucked away in the corner.

I glanced at the key in my hand and then at the door.

"Worth a shot," I muttered, trudging over to the door and slipping the key into the lock.

It turned easily, the door swinging open with a soft creak. I stepped through, expecting another hallway or maybe a room. But no. I stepped out into... something else entirely.

The sky was pink. *Pink*. And the grass—well, it wasn't exactly grass. It shimmered, like a rainbow made out of thousands of tiny crystals, each one catching the light and sparkling in ways that couldn't be real.

"What the actual hell is this?" I whispered, taking a few hesitant steps forward. The trees around me were tall, their branches heavy with strange, oddly shaped fruits. Some of them looked like they belonged on Earth. Others... not so much.

I stared up at the sky, the impossible colors swirling above me like a kaleidoscope, and I couldn't help but laugh. "Someone definitely slipped me acid," I muttered. That was the only explanation, right? Some kind of weird trip. A dream. Anything but real life.

I sighed, shaking my head. "Okay, Alice. Time to figure out where the hell you are. And more importantly, how the hell to get out."

But as I stared at the shimmering landscape in front of me, a small voice in the back of my head whispered that maybe—just maybe—I wasn't going to wake up from this one.

CHAPTER THREE

I ambled along the vibrant path, absorbing the lush, unnatural beauty around me, when that familiar white blur—the rabbit—appeared again. It darted off the path, beckoning me into unknown territories. I knew better, I really did. But the curiosity that had led me to this bizarre world wasn't about to let a little wisdom get in the way now.

As I followed the white rabbit, weaving through an array of bizarrely colored trees, my foot caught on a hidden root. The world tilted dangerously. Panic clawed at my chest as the ground seemed to fall away beneath me. My arms flailed, grabbing at the air, as I pitched forward down a steep embankment. The descent was a chaotic blur of scratching branches and sharp stones that sent adrenaline surging through my veins like wildfire.

I crashed into the river with a shock that drove the breath from my lungs. The cold embrace of the water was a brutal awakening, grappling with the air in my lungs as I kicked desperately for the surface. Murky water blurred my vision, the current tugging at me, threatening to pull me back under. When my head finally broke free, I gasped, dragging the damp, heavy air into my chest.

Drenched and disoriented, I swam to the riverbank and clambered out. My heart pounded against my ribs, adrenaline still coursing through me as I stood there, water streaming from my clothes, pooling at my feet. The one thing I loathe—wet clothes clinging coldly to my skin.

With a huff, I trekked back to the path I'd strayed from, irritation prickling at every soaked step. "Great, just my luck to end up soaking wet in a land that probably doesn't even have towels," I muttered to myself. Then, a rueful smile tugged at my lips, "Or me someone who'd appreciate my dirty sense of humor."

Seeing no one around in this bizarre slice of the world, I decided to make the best of the sun's warmth. I stripped off my makeshift dress, draping it over a branch. There I was, standing naked under a foreign sky. It felt... exhilarating. Liberating and oddly arousing to be so vulnerable yet so unseen. I laid down on a patch of grass that sparkled under the sun, letting the strange, ticklish blades caress my bare skin.

"Anyone there?" I called out, half-expecting an answer. Silence greeted me, and I smiled, leaning back. My fingers began tracing idle, wandering paths across my skin, from my neck down to the curves of my breasts. The sensation was intoxicating—a blend of danger and desire, making my breath hitch.

I couldn't deny the heat building within me, an insistent pulse that demanded attention. My hand slipped lower, fingers exploring, stirring the warmth between my thighs into a fiery need. My touch was both question and answer, and as I found my slick, eager center, a low moan slipped from my lips.

"Fuck, that's good," I murmured to myself, my words a husky whisper against the backdrop of this strange, silent world. Alone, unseen, I let my inhibitions melt away like mist under the morning sun.

My gaze, heavy with desire, caught on a long, purple fruit dangling enticingly from a nearby tree. Its shape, unabashedly phallic, called to something primal within me. "Might as well see what all the fuss is about," I thought aloud, the words tinged with a playful curiosity as I reached for the fruit. It was firm, yet yielding, its surface ridged in a way that promised new depths of pleasure.

Clutching the fruit, I settled back into the grass, spreading my thighs wide to welcome this new companion. The initial touch of the cool fruit against my hot, flushed skin sent a shiver through me. "Oh, fuck yes," I exhaled as I guided it towards my dripping entrance. The cold was a sharp contrast, but as I slid the fruit inside, a delicious warmth began to spread through me, filling me, pushing me toward a precipice I hadn't known I was standing on.

I moved it slowly at first, savoring the sensation of being filled so completely. "Deeper," I gasped, urging myself on, my movements growing more urgent, more desperate. My free hand darted down to my clit, fingers circling with a fervor that matched the rhythmic thrusting of the fruit. "Yes, just like that," I moaned, the words spilling out in a breathy litany as I built myself toward climax.

My body tensed, the sensation coiling tightly within me, ready to snap. "I'm gonna come," I whispered fiercely, a declaration to the empty air. The pleasure mounted, overwhelming, consuming, until it broke over me in a wild, explosive release that left me gasping, undone by my own hands, under the watchful eye of this alien sky.

As I lay there, breathless and basking in the afterglow, the reality of my solitude melded with the intensity of my release, leaving me with a sense of daring fulfillment that was as intoxicating as it was liberating.

It was only as I lay there, catching my breath, that I noticed—I wasn't alone. My eyes snapped open to find myself under scrutiny, the intensity of the gaze unmistakable even from a distance.

CHAPTER FOUR

I stood abruptly, my heart racing as I realized I was no longer alone. Clumsily, I stumbled over myself, my cheeks flushing with heat as I reached for my now-dry dress strewn across the nearby branch. Pulling it on quickly, I turned to face the intruder.

There he was, a vision of absurdity and allure. His hot pink suit was a size too small, straining against muscles that seemed carved from marble, while his mustard yellow pants were an audacious choice that somehow worked. He wore a patchwork top hat, tilted jauntily over dark, tousled hair. His caramel skin and green eyes framed by a spray of freckles across his nose made him look like an artwork come to life.

I ran my fingers through my hair, trying to

appear somewhat presentable despite the circumstances. This man had witnessed me fuck my pussy, and yet, there was no judgment in his eyes, only an intense curiosity that seemed to strip me bare once again.

He sauntered closer, each step a testament to his confident, almost predatory grace. With a flourish, he tipped his hat and bowed deeply. "Good day," he intoned with a smirk.

"Hello," I managed, voice wavering as I dipped into an awkward curtsy. "I was just, um…" My words trailed off, a pathetic attempt to explain my earlier indiscretion.

"No need for excuses here," he interrupted, his voice as smooth as velvet. "We're all mad in our own ways."

He ran his tongue along his lips, it was predatory and utterly mesmerizing. "My name is Hector Maddox, but my friends call me Hat."

"Alice," I replied, feeling the weight of his gaze like a physical touch.

"Alice," he repeated, savoring each syllable as if tasting a fine wine. "Such a lovely name for a lovely girl."

I felt a flush creep up my neck. "Were you headed somewhere?" I asked, eager to change the subject.

"Indeed, I was on my way to a tea party," he said, eyes twinkling with mischief. "You must join me. It's not every day we get to feast with such... enticing company."

His words excited me, his gaze heavy with unspoken promises. I realized then just how hungry I was—not just for food but for the adventure he offered.

He seemed to read my thoughts, a sly smile playing on his lips. "Come, let's indulge in the madness together."

Without waiting for a formal agreement, he offered his arm, which I took, my body tingling with anticipation. As we began to walk, he did something wholly unexpected—instead of a dignified stroll, he began to skip, pulling me along in a whimsical dance down the path.

"Life is far too important to be taken seriously," he quipped as we skipped, his laughter like music.

As we moved through this lush, outlandish version of Wonderland, every sense was heightened. The colors seemed brighter, the sounds more melodious, and on the air was the delicate scent of blooming flowers and something more intoxicating —desire.

"So, Alice," Hat began, his voice low and inviting, "tell me something true about yourself."

"I'm usually not one for outdoor escapades," I confessed, feeling daring under his gaze.

"Ah, but today seems to be a day for shattering norms," he countered, his eyes gleaming with challenge.

As we approached the venue of the tea party, the whimsy of this wonderland unfurled before us in a breathtaking spectacle. The table, a long stretch of solid dark wood, was resplendent with flowers painted in a riot of colors that seemed to dance in the dappled sunlight. It rested under an avenue of trees from which odd trinkets and fruits dangled, swaying gently in the breeze.

Upon closer inspection, I noticed among the trinkets were fruits of the same purple variety I had encountered earlier. My cheeks flushed at the memory. Not far from them hung a cluster of pink fruits, their elongated, beaded structure reminiscent of anal beads, sparking a flutter of curiosity within me.

As I took my seat, it became apparent that the guests at this gathering were all men, each adorned in elaborately colorful suits that defied the drab conventions of the ordinary world. Their attire shimmered with sequins and silks, making them look like princes from a particularly decadent court.

The first to introduce himself was a man in a

peacock-blue suit with emerald green accents that matched his eyes. "I'm Jasper," he said, his voice smooth and enticing. "And I do hope you find the party... stimulating." His suggestive wink made me think of tangled sheets and whispered secrets.

Next to him sat a man, clad in a suit of deep violet with gold pinstripes. His dark hair was slicked back, and his eyes, a piercing slate gray, seemed to strip me down to my barest desires. "Elliot. Charmed, I'm sure," he murmured, his gaze lingering on me in a way that suggested he was imagining much more than just polite conversation.

On his other side was a man who introduced himself as Lucas. His suit was a brilliant shade of sunburst orange. His tousled blonde hair and easy smile gave him an approachable air, but the mischievous glint in his eye promised devilish fun. "Alice, lovely to meet a girl who knows how to enjoy the fruits of Wonderland," he joked, gesturing subtly to the hanging fruits with a playful raise of his eyebrows.

Completing the quartet was Nathaniel, wearing a suit of rich crimson that set off his dark skin and jet-black hair. His smile was slow and knowing, the kind that suggested he was well-versed in the art of pleasure. "Welcome to our little escape from reality," he said with a voice that caressed all the right nerves.

As we settled in, I found my gaze roaming from one man to the next, each more intriguing and attractive than the last. The air was intoxicating—lusty. The table was laden with an array of dishes that were as colorful and exotic as the men themselves, each plate promising a sensory overload.

Hat leaned closer, his breath tickling my ear. "Prepare yourself, Alice. This tea party is like none you've ever attended. Here, we feast on more than just food." His words, laced with a husky undertone, sent shivers down my spine.

The realization dawned on me: this wasn't just a feast for the stomach but for the senses, a playground of desires laid bare under the guise of a tea party. Each man seemed to offer a different temptation, a promise of pleasures untold.

As we took our seats among the madcap revelers, anticipation vibrated in the air. Promises were whispered in glances that undressed any façade I still had up. I knew one thing for certain: I was exactly where I needed to be, on the brink of indulging in the most decadent of delights.

CHAPTER FIVE

As the tea party continued, the men around me whispered to each other, their voices a low hum beneath the clinking of teacups and laughter. My plate was an artist's palette of whimsical treats: mini sandwiches in funny shapes, brightly colored cookies, and cupcakes that looked too pretty to eat. Four cups of tea sat before me, each one a different shade of absurdity. Choosing the hot pink teacup with bright yellow flowers painted on it, I couldn't help but giggle at the sheer extravagance of it all.

Jasper, noticing my amusement, rose from his high-backed wooden chair and approached with a confidence that made my heart skip. "Would you like to take a stroll through the garden, Alice?" he asked, his voice a smooth invitation into the unknown.

"Carpe diem," I replied, embracing the spirit of adventure. He offered his hand with a gallant bend, and as I placed mine in his, he spun me behind his back and scooped me up onto his shoulders. His touch was a surprise, goosing my bum playfully, sending a delightful shiver through me. His strength was palpable; I felt weightless against his muscular frame. As he hopped forward, each bounce sent thrilling vibrations to my center, the friction stirring a delicious warmth within me.

The garden that unfolded before us was a vivid tapestry of colors, predominantly red with roses so deeply hued they seemed almost unreal. "It's beautiful," I breathed, lost in the enchantment of the place.

Jasper set me down gently among the flowers, his hands lingering just a moment too long on my hips. "We're in a little subsection of the Fae realm called Wonderland," he explained, his voice lowering as he guided me through the blooms. "And it's all ruled by the Red Queen. She's... formidable, to say the least, and not one to be crossed."

The way he spoke of the queen sent a chill down my spine. "What happens if you break her rules?" I asked, my voice barely above a whisper.

"Death," he replied somberly. "She does not take kindly to disobedience."

Despite the warning, the danger seemed distant, almost like part of a game—one I was more than willing to play. Jasper's closeness was intoxicating, his every touch sending chills down my spine. He played with a strand of my hair, his fingers skilled and teasing. "What's your favorite flower?" he asked suddenly.

I glanced around at the vibrant display surrounding us. "I've always been a fan of lavender," I confessed, the scent already mingling in the air, subtle yet pervasive.

Jasper smiled, his eyes glinting with mischief. "A choice as enchanting as you are, Alice." He gestured expansively to the garden around us. "Here, the Red Queen prefers the red roses—she believes they symbolize the strength and blood of her reign. Picking one without permission is said to bring... certain doom."

His words hung between us, laden with an unspoken warning. Yet, as my eyes caught the brilliant red of the roses, curiosity overcame caution. I reached out and plucked a single rose, its petals as soft as velvet against my fingers. Jasper watched me, a curious expression on his face, but he said nothing about my bold move.

"The Red Queen sounds terrifying," I murmured, twirling the rose by its stem.

"She can be, but Wonderland is full of secrets and delights that often outweigh the dangers," Jasper replied, drawing closer. His hand brushed mine, sending a jolt of electricity through me. "Would you like to explore some of those delights with me?" His voice was a velvet caress, promising pleasures untold.

"When in Rome—or Wonderland," I laughed softly, the thrill of the unknown coursing through me. "Lead the way."

Jasper offered a roguish grin and led me deeper into the garden. "Wonderland has a way of amplifying everything—feelings, sensations... desires." He plucked a sprig of lavender and handed it to me. "Smell this, and tell me if it doesn't make the world seem brighter."

I inhaled deeply, the familiar, soothing scent of lavender filling my senses, making the colors of the garden seem even more vivid. "It's wonderful," I sighed, a smile spreading across my face.

"And it's just the beginning," Jasper murmured. His fingers traced a line down my arm, raising goosebumps. "Imagine what other sensations await."

Captivated by his words and the promise in his

eyes, I nodded, eager to experience everything he was offering. As he leaned in, his breath warm against my cheek, he whispered, "Let's find a more secluded spot, where I can show you just how pleasurable Wonderland can be."

I looked him up and down, taking in the strength in his frame and the mischievous spark in his eyes. "Yes, a thousand percent yes," I said.

With that, Jasper took my hand, leading me through the maze of flowers and scents, towards a hidden alcove draped in wisteria. The world seemed to fall away, leaving only the promise of ecstasy, the danger of the queen's rules a distant thought against the backdrop of impending delight.

He handed me the flowers, and as I inhaled deeply, the world around us seemed to shimmer even brighter. Jasper traced a finger down my arm, raising goosebumps on my skin. "Come to me, Alice," he beckoned, leading me deeper into the garden.

I followed, plucking a red rose along the way, and soon found myself in a field of lavender under a pink, swirling sky. Laying back among the fragrant blooms, Jasper produced a peacock feather as if from thin air and began to trace it along my arms, neck, and back.

"Your beauty is unparalleled, Alice," he whispered, his voice heavy with desire. "Every curve, every breath... I want to explore all of you."

Encouraged by his words, I let my makeshift dress fall away, feeling bold and utterly captivated. He watched me with intense appreciation, a deep chuckle escaping him. "Do you want to wear my hat?" he teased, offering it to me with a playful grin.

Slipping the hat on, it fell over my eyes, and I giggled, feeling like a character in our own private play. "Is it okay if I kiss you?" he murmured, his breath hot against my skin.

"Yes," I breathed out eagerly, pulling the hat up to meet his lips.

"But I didn't want to kiss you there," he teased, his lips wandering to my neck, then lower, each kiss igniting a fire within me. He worshipped my body with his mouth, exploring each part of me with a reverent intensity. When he reached my hips, he paused, his breath warm against my mound.

Spreading my legs, I invited him closer, and he didn't hesitate. His tongue found my heat, teasing at my slit before focusing on my clit. The sensation was overwhelming, a crescendo of pleasure that built with every flick and suck.

"I need more," I gasped, lost in the sensation and desperate for him to fill me.

Jasper looked up, his eyes dark with desire that seemed to capture the very essence of twilight. "I thought you'd never ask," he murmured, his voice a low rumble that vibrated through my very core. He positioned himself between my thighs, his presence electrifying. As he entered me, the world seemed to shift into a spectrum of pulsing colors. The sky above us blazed with hues of pink and violet, each shade shimmering in time with our rhythm. It was an orchestra of light and sensation, unlike anything I had ever experienced.

Every touch was intensified by the magic of this place, every movement resonated through my body like a chord struck on a celestial harp. Jasper moved with a purposeful grace, exploring every contour of my being, his hands tracing the arcs and valleys of my form as if he were learning a sacred text.

As he drove deeper, a coiling tension wound its way through my limbs, anchoring me to the spot, yet urging me to soar. I felt it in my clenched toes, in my arched back, in the breath that I held tight within my lungs. The world narrowed to the point of exquisite pressure where our bodies joined, each thrust pushing me closer to the edge of an abyss I yearned to tumble into.

He whispered promises, each one a vow to take

me higher, to push me further into the realm of ecstasy. "I'm going to make you come," he assured, his voice thick with the power of impending fulfillment. His words were both a command and an invocation, summoning a climax that built like a storm on the horizon.

The sky seemed to shutter with color, a kaleidoscope that mirrored the crescendo of sensations that overwhelmed me. It was incredible, a symphony of light and touch that stole the very breath from my lungs. I had never done drugs, but I imagined no high could possibly compare to the intensity of this moment. The world spun, the colors danced, and I was adrift in a sea of pleasure so profound it seemed to transcend the boundaries of reality.

With a final, deep thrust, he sent me spiraling over the edge. My climax washed over me in waves, each one a crashing surge that left me shuddering and gasping. Jasper held me close as I trembled, his arms a fortress against the quaking of my limbs, his breath a warm caress against the shell of my ear.

"We're here together, in this wonder," he whispered, his lips brushing against my skin, imprinting his words like a seal upon my heart.

As we lay there, wrapped in each other's arms among the fragrant lavender and roses, the garden around us seemed to settle, as if it too had been caught up in our storm. A profound peace enveloped us, and in that serene aftermath, I knew that Wonderland had claimed not just a piece of my heart, but whispered promises of belonging that I was only just beginning to understand.

CHAPTER SIX

The return to the tea party found me feeling ravenous, as though my earlier exploits with Jasper had awakened not just new desires but a profound hunger as well. I glanced at the ornate clock perched near the spread of treats— it stubbornly marked six o'clock, just as it had when I first arrived.

"Is it still tea time?" I asked, a hint of amusement coloring my tone.

"It's always six o'clock here. Not time for anything else but tea, and enjoying the company of those around us," Hat quipped, his smile infectious.

Laughing, I decided to simply surrender to the whimsy of this place. I indulged in the spread before me: sandwiches layered with exotic, vibrant fillings that melted on the tongue, cookies dotted with unknown but delicious bits, and a peculiar gelatin dessert that shimmered under the light. Each bite was a discovery, a celebration of flavors so decadent that they seemed to dance on my palate. I sipped on a tea that was a curious blend of sweet and spicy, its steam carrying tales of distant, spicy shores.

After gloriously gorging, I patted my stomach, slightly overwhelmed by the feast. "I need to walk off this full tummy," I stood with a slight groan of contentment.

Elliot, who had been quietly observing from the edge of the gathering, rose smoothly to his feet. "May I suggest a stroll by the lake? It's quite a sight under the moonlight," he offered, his voice carrying the soft promise.

Intrigued, I nodded.

Elliot led me down a winding path that seemed to be lit by the natural luminescence of the night itself. As we approached the lake, the sight took my breath away. Not one, but three moons hung in the sky, each casting a different gentle light onto the landscape: one silver, another pale blue, and the third a soft, ghostly green. The reflections danced across the water's surface in a mesmerizing ballet of light.

"The moons of Wonderland," Elliot began, his voice smooth as velvet in the tranquil night, "are more than celestial bodies; they are the source of our realm's magic. Each moon influences different elements of our world and ourselves. They can amplify emotions, enhance sensations, and even manipulate time."

"They are said to reflect not just light, but the very essence of those who gaze upon them. What do you see in their reflection, Alice?"

I peered into the lake, watching the triple reflections ripple and transform with the gentle lapping of the water. "I see... possibility," I murmured, captivated by the shifting patterns.

Elliot nodded, a smile playing at the corners of his mouth. "Possibility is a powerful thing. It can shape empires, and it can define who we choose to be," he said, his gaze intense as it met mine. "In Wonderland, we are often who we believe ourselves to be, reflected back at us in myriad ways."

His words wove through the cool night air, crafting an atmosphere thick with introspection. "And who do you believe yourself to be, Alice, here in this place of eternal tea parties and moonlit lakes?"

I was silent for a moment, considering his question. It was one thing to play along with the madness of Wonderland, but another to confront what this world was mirroring about my innermost self. "I think... I'm someone who's looking for more than what I've known. Someone who's not afraid to explore who I might be."

"Exploration is an art," Elliot responded, his voice soft yet compelling. "And like all art, it requires both courage and vulnerability. Here by this lake, under the gaze of three moons, you can dare to explore, to see the parts of yourself that you hide from the world."

"Wonderland is a reflection, Alice. It shows us not just what we are, but what we can become." Elliot stepped closer, his presence enveloping. "What do you want to become?"

Captivated, I watched as the moonlight played on the lake, its surface shimmering with the magic that Elliot described. "How does the magic influence all this?" I gestured to the expanse of the lake and the vibrant flora surrounding us.

Elliot smiled, a knowing twinkle in his eye. "Watch." He guided me to a cluster of roses, bathed in the tri-moonlight, their red petals so deep they were nearly black. "These roses thrive under the moon's magic. Smell one, but remember—just smell, don't pluck. Their scent is intoxicating, enhanced by the moons to heighten all of your senses."

Tentatively, I leaned in and inhaled the fragrance

of a rose. The effect was immediate and profound; my skin tingled as if the petals themselves were brushing against me, and every sound and color around me seemed amplified. The magic of the moons made the world around me vibrate with an intensity that was almost palpable.

Elliot's hand found the small of my back, sending a jolt of electricity through me. "Embrace what Wonderland has to offer," he murmured into my ear, his breath warm against my neck.

As he traced invisible lines down my arms, his touch sparked trails of goosebumps, heightening my already sensitized skin. He stepped closer, and I could feel the heat of his body even without direct contact. Encouraged by his closeness, I reached back, my hands finding the contours of his form through his clothes. My fingers brushed against the outline of his arousal, and I grasped him gently, confirming what my body already knew—he wanted me as much as I did him.

With a fluid motion, I let my makeshift dress fall to the ground, the fabric whispering against my skin as it pooled at my feet. I bent forward, the position exposing me to the cool night air and to Elliot's gaze. He caressed my buttocks, his hands strong yet gentle, before slipping a finger along my wetness. His touch was expert, knowing, sending waves of pleasure coursing through me as he found my most sensitive spots.

Elliot's voice was low, almost reverent as he whispered, "You're exquisite, Alice. Every inch of you responds so beautifully." He encouraged my hips back towards him, and I felt his hardness teasing at my entrance.

"I need to feel you inside of me," I breathed out, the desire clear in my voice.

"That's the roses talking," he teased, his breath hot against my ear.

"I was ready to fuck you the first time I laid eyes on you," I shot back, the boldness of the environment emboldening me further.

Without another word, he entered me, his thrusts deliberate and deep. Each movement was synchronized with the pulsating light of the moons, each stroke pushing us both toward a climax that seemed to be written in the stars above. As he brushed against my puckered hole with his thumb, I gasped, the sensation new and electrifying.

"More," I begged, and he obliged by slipping his thumb inside, slowly stretching me in ways that had my entire body trembling. The world around us seemed to explode in a crescendo of moonlit ecstasy as I came, waves of intense pleasure radiating from where we joined to every extremity.

Laying there by the reflective lake, under the watchful eyes of the three moons, wrapped in the arms of Elliot, I knew Wonderland wasn't just a place, but a state of being—transformative, magical, and utterly intoxicating.

CHAPTER SEVEN

"Time really is just a suggestion here, isn't it?" I asked, my tone laced with amusement as Hat topped off my tea with a flourish.

"It's always six o'clock," Lucas chimed in with a wink.

Feeling delightfully sated by the food and tea, I pushed back from the table with a groan of contentment.

Lucas rose, offering his hand with a gallant flair. "Allow me to guide you through our rose maze. It's not just a walk; it's an experience." His voice was a seductive whisper.

Intrigued by the anticipation in his eyes, I followed him into a labyrinth where the air was a perfume of roses and mystery. "Each turn holds a surprise," Lucas explained as we approached the first corner.

He paused and produced a pair of benwa balls from his pocket, their silver surface gleaming seductively. "These will enhance every step you take," he murmured, his voice low and enticing as he placed them in my hand. His fingers brushed against mine, sending a shivers up my arm.

With a mix of excitement and a flush of daring, I allowed him to guide me in inserting the benwa balls. The sensation was immediate—a delicious, subtle pressure that promised to build with each step. "You'll find they add quite the thrill to our little journey," he assured me, a wicked grin playing across his lips.

As we ventured deeper into the maze, the path turned and revealed a new surprise. Lucas stopped before a pair of delicate nipple clamps adorned with tiny roses. "These will sharpen your pleasure," he explained, his hands deftly applying the clamps. The slight pinch was a perfect echo to the internal sensations, and a dual wave of pleasure began to pulse through me.

Another turn brought us to a mysterious setup: a bar with cuffs. "For a touch of restraint," he whispered, his breath hot against my ear as he secured my ankles, spreading me open with an intimacy that drew a gasp from my lips.

The vulnerability was exhilarating, heightening the sensations that the maze conjured within me. I was open, exposed, and teetering on the edge of overwhelming pleasure. "Lucas, please," I found myself begging, a desperate need to climax building within me.

With a predatory smile, Lucas knelt before me. He lifted my cuffed legs slightly, his tongue finding my eager clit. The world narrowed to the point of his tongue and the relentless pressure of the benwa balls. His mouth was skilled, each flick and suckle pushing me closer to the brink.

"More, please," I gasped, lost in the sensation.

In a swift motion, Lucas stood, releasing his arousal. He entered me in one fluid thrust, filling me completely, intensifying the sensation of the benwa balls inside me. I dug my fingers into the earth as he moved, each thrust more insistent than the last. His rhythm was relentless, and when he brought me to climax, I screamed, a raw sound of intense release that echoed off the maze walls.

But one climax wasn't enough for Lucas. He kept moving, building me up swiftly again. As he thrust, he rubbed my clit, pushing me over into another explosive orgasm. His own climax followed, marked by a groan of release as he filled me with his warmth.

Afterwards, Lucas gently removed the benwa balls, the cuffs, and the nipple clamps, each movement tender and caring. He held me close, his voice soft and full of wonder. "You're incredible, Alice. Absolutely magical."

In Lucas's arms, amidst the tangled paths of the rose maze, I realized that Wonderland wasn't just a place of whimsy and madness—it was a realm where every hidden desire could come to life, where every fantasy was just around the corner, waiting to be discovered and explored.

CHAPTER EIGHT

Back at the tea table, the world of Wonderland sprawled around us like a canvas of absurd delights. Here, sex toys sprouted on trees as naturally as apples, and laughter seemed to bubble up from the very ground. The vibrant, surreal landscape was a playground for the senses, where happiness wasn't just around every corner—it practically paved the streets.

I indulged in more of the exotic, tantalizing, sometimes phallic food, each bite a burst of joy on my tongue. The tea party was in full swing, the air carried on it the rich aroma of spiced tea and the sound of carefree conversations.

"You know," I started, a mischievous glint in my eye, "I wish Wonderland had a playground. Swinging sounds like such fun here."

Hat, always quick on the uptake, exchanged a knowing look with Nathaniel. "Oh, but we do have a playground," he said, his voice laced with double entendre. "Perhaps a little stroll to stretch our legs?"

Nathaniel's smile was slow and seductive. "Indeed, it's not far. A place to really swing to your heart's content," he added, the twinkle in his eyes unmistakable.

Intrigued and more than a little excited by the prospect, I agreed, and we set off down a path that seemed to beckon us forward with its clear, inviting trail. It led us to an adult playspace that redefined the concept of a playground. Traditional swings were replaced with luxurious sex swings, and there were artfully arranged stations for bondage, complete with silky ropes and elegant restraints.

The sight of the elaborate setups, designed for all manner of pleasurable pursuits, had my body tingling with anticipation. The thought of being with both Hat and Nathaniel in such an environment sent a rush of heat through me.

As we entered, the rules of this playspace were clear—consent was paramount, each action and gesture needing affirmation. Hat turned to me, his gaze intense. "Do you consent to exploring your boundaries with us, Alice?" he asked, his voice both commanding and caring.

With a nod, I gave my permission, excitement coursing through me at the prospect of such an adventure. Nathaniel stepped forward, his presence just as commanding. "And I submit to your desires as well, Alice. Guide us through your fantasies."

The dynamic of control shifted fluidly between us. Hat directed me with a firm yet respectful tone. "Undress, Alice," he instructed, watching intently as I complied. "Yes, sir," I responded, feeling a thrill at the command.

Soon, I was strapped into a sex swing, the cool air of Wonderland kissing my bare skin. Hat and Nathaniel adjusted the straps, ensuring I was comfortable yet completely exposed. Hat, noticing my flushed cheeks and quick breath, praised me, "You're such a good girl, Alice." I realized then how much his approval exhilarated me.

With my consent, Hat blindfolded me, plunging my world into darkness. The absence of sight heightened my other senses to an almost unbearable intensity. I felt a feather-like caress trail up my inner thighs, teasing over my skin and sending shivers through my body.

Then, without warning, a firmer touch snapped a whip against my buttocks. The sting was startling yet strangely delightful. As I rocked back and forth on the swing, the blend of pain and pleasure melded into a symphony of sensations.

A warm breath teased my ear before a tongue lavished attention on my throbbing clit. The rhythmic licking pushed me to the brink of ecstasy. "Please, more," I gasped, desperate for the fulfillment only a cock could provide.

uddenly, fulfilling my plea, someone—his identity obscured by the blindfold's darkness—thrust into me. His cock drove deep, each movement forceful yet calculated, as if he were both claiming and worshipping my body with each stroke. The intensity of his thrusts catapulted me over the edge into a staggering, all-consuming orgasm. My body arched instinctively, straining against the soft constraints of the swing, as wave after wave of pleasure crashed over me. My breath caught in bursts, my voice a crescendo of gasps and moans that filled the air.

As the waves of my climax ebbed into satisfying aftershocks, I reached up and yanked off the blindfold, the sudden return of light momentarily disorienting. My eyes focused, and there he was—Hat, his expression one of intense satisfaction mixed with tender care. His body still joined with mine, he smiled down at me, his cock still erect, pulsing gently inside me. With a grace that spoke of deep familiarity, he began to kiss his way up my body. Each kiss was a seal of the pleasure we shared, starting from my thighs and moving upwards, igniting tiny fires on my skin wherever his lips touched.

Breathless and still reeling from the heights we had reached, I turned my gaze towards Nathaniel, who had been watching us with a look of intense desire etched across his features. "Lick me clean," I commanded, my voice thick with the remnants of pleasure and the authority of newfound desires awakened in this Wonderland's embrace.

Nathaniel moved forward without hesitation, his movements eager and fluid. He knelt between my widely spread legs, his eyes locked on mine as he leaned in. His tongue, skilled and warm, met the sensitive flesh still pulsing from my recent climax. He licked delicately at first, savoring the mix of our mingled juices, before his actions became more purposeful—his tongue drawing broad, firm strokes designed to rekindle the fire that had barely begun to wane.

The sensation of being cleaned by such a devoted, attentive mouth was profoundly erotic, sending ripples of pleasure coursing through once again. Nathaniel's dedication to the task, his eagerness to taste and please, drew me rapidly back to a peak of arousal. Just as I felt myself nearing the brink once more, he paused, his gaze intense and questioning, seeking permission for something more.

With a nod, I invited him to continue, and he shifted his position. Aligning himself with the entrance of my still-throbbing center, he entered me smoothly, his cock sliding in with an ease born of our combined slickness. Nathaniel filled me completely, his strokes deep and sure, pushing me further into a spiral of ecstasy. Each thrust was a perfect counterpoint to Hat's earlier fervor, and together, they played me like an instrument tuned to the key of pleasure.

Nathaniel's pace quickened, his movements becoming more urgent as he drove us both toward another explosive climax. The sensation of being so thoroughly possessed, so deeply cherished by these two men, was overwhelming. When the climax broke over me, it was with a force that blurred the edges of reality, the pleasure so intense that for a moment, I wondered if I had transcended into another realm entirely.

After the waves of ecstasy had finally subsided, leaving me languid and utterly spent, Nathaniel gently withdrew. Both he and Hat, with careful and tender motions, helped me out of the swing, their arms supporting me as my legs trembled with residual pleasure. Hat's embrace enveloped me, his strength a comforting presence as he carried me away from the playground, cradling me against his chest.

As we left the adult playspace behind, the echoes of our shared ecstasy lingered in the air, a sweet melody of fulfilled desires and explored boundaries that promised even more wonders in the days to come in Wonderland.

CHAPTER NINE

The roses had seemed harmless enough, and I'd indulged in picking them without a second thought. Their vibrant colors, the velvet-soft petals between my fingers—it had all felt like a simple pleasure, a small rebellion against the strangeness of Wonderland. But now, as I stand here and face the Queen's knight, the weight of my actions settles over me like a shroud.

The knight regards me with an impassive stare, his presence as imposing as the armored horses I'd seen galloping through Wonderland's gardens. "Alice, by order of the Queen of Hearts, you're to remain here until she arrives," he declares, his tone leaving no room for negotiation. "She'll be arriving promptly at six o'clock."

I glance at the clock tower, but it's always six

here, always teatime. I swallow, a hint of unease curling through me as the knight lifts a trumpet to his lips, the piercing notes announcing the Queen's impending arrival. It dawns on me that, perhaps, I'd underestimated Wonderland's rules—and the consequences of breaking them.

The Queen of Hearts enters in a rush of color and presence, sweeping into the room with a fluid grace that borders on lethal. She's taller than I imagined, wearing a scarlet ballgown that plunges down to an innie belly button, long red hair cascading over bare shoulders. She is, without a doubt, the most stunning woman I have ever seen. There's a dark allure to her, a power that prickles across my skin and sends a shiver through me.

Around me, the Hatters drop to their knees, bowing their heads in reverence, and I realize with growing unease that I am the only one left standing. A guard to my left growls, "Kneel before your Queen!"

It takes a beat for me to understand they're talking to me, and I falter, pointing to myself as if to clarify. The Queen steps forward, her lips curling into a smirk as she regards me with an intensity that makes my stomach flip.

"Alice of Wonderland," she begins, only for me to interrupt her.

"I'm not from Wonderland," I say quickly, but my words barely matter.

The Queen tilts her head, amusement flickering in her eyes. "Alice in Wonderland, you plucked my roses, and now you refuse to kneel? You're a bold one." She raises a finger and brushes it along my cheek, then tilts my chin up, forcing me to meet her gaze. "I am your Queen."

The words come sharp, cutting through the air with an authority that makes me tingle. I open my mouth to protest, but she holds up a hand, stopping me.

"For this offense, I think a fitting punishment is in order. I believe three roses were plucked, yes? Three times, then, shall you be punished."

A rush of heat blooms in my cheeks, but I nod, letting my gaze fall. I'm mesmerized by the challenge in her eyes, by the sharpness of her presence. "I accept your punishment," I murmur, not entirely sure what to expect.

She steps closer, guiding me over to the table. I bend over at her silent command, my breath hitching as she lifts my skirt. The room feels charged, like we're at the edge of a thunderstorm. Her breath is warm against my ear as she leans in, her voice low and sultry. "You've been a very bad girl, Alice. Plucking my roses, flouting my laws. You deserve to be taught a lesson."

"How bad was I?" I ask, surprised by the anticipation in my own voice.

"Oh, terrible," she purrs, running a hand along my backside. "You'll think twice before touching what's mine."

Her palm lands on my bare skin, a sharp, stinging slap that leaves me gasping. The pain blurs into pleasure, and I arch my back, pressing into her touch as she strokes the place she just struck. Her hand moves slowly, teasing over the curve of my hips, then down further, fingers trailing across my inner thighs and pressing into my slick heat. My body shudders as she runs her fingers along the length of me, finding me wet and wanting. She knows it, too, and I can feel her smile against my neck as she traces delicate circles over my clit, making me gasp.

My moans echo finding the ears of every onlooker, her fingers skillfully teasing my body, drawing me closer to the edge. Just as I think I might lose myself in the sensation, she pulls back, only to bring her palm down on me again, harder this time. I cry out, a mixture of shock and pleasure spilling from my lips.

The Queen doesn't pause. Her fingers slip back

between my legs, pushing into me, filling me. I let out a strangled moan, my body curling into her touch, heat coiling deep in my belly as she moves, relentless and controlled. Her other hand presses down on my back, pinning me in place as she parts my legs and enters me further. Her fingers thrust deep, then slow, twisting inside me as she drives me closer to the brink.

My breath hitches, and I can feel myself beginning to unravel, but just before I reach the peak, she withdraws, leaving me empty and aching. Another slap lands on my backside, sharper this time, and I yelp, feeling the sting race up my spine.

"You've taken three roses," she murmurs, her voice like silk over gravel, "so I'll make sure you're thoroughly punished for each." She trails her hand over my thighs, her fingers finding my clit again, rubbing in circles that send shivers through me. Her other hand cups my breast, squeezing just enough to make me gasp. She leans in, her breath hot on my ear. "If you ever touch my roses again, I'll see to it that you never feel the hot rush of pleasure again."

I let out a strangled moan, hips bucking into her touch. The world fades away until it's just us, her fingers working me, her presence filling every corner of my senses. She's close, so close I can feel the warmth of her body against mine, and her scent surrounds me, intoxicating and heady.

When she pulls back, it's like being doused in ice water, but before I can protest, she lifts me upright and hands me a cool rag. I shake my head, declining it, not wanting to break the spell just yet.

"Good," she purrs, and then her lips are on mine, soft but insistent. I can taste her, feel her, every nerve alight as she pulls away, leaving me breathless, suspended on the edge of something I can't quite name.

CHAPTER TEN

The Queen of Hearts had swept away, her regal presence leaving the air thick with lingering tension. The Hatters, as if freed from an enchantment, picked up right where they'd left off, pouring tea into chipped cups and chattering as if nothing had happened. I watched them for a moment, their laughter strangely hollow in my ears, and felt an odd sense of disconnection. It was like I was slipping back into myself, as if I'd been pulled out of a trance.

I traced my fingers over the ring on my hand, the delicate band warm against my skin. A shiver of déjà vu rippled through me as I recognized the faint etching along its surface. Memories flooded back, bringing with them the scent of herbs and old wood, and Rainbow's voice from the jewelry store—Lilly

Drake—floating in my mind like a forgotten warning.

The name came back to me: Lilly Drake. Rainbow had been so clear, hadn't she? She'd said something about the ring's power and the caution it required. I recalled her exact words now: "The rings don't always let you go back if they're not done with you." I gazed around at Wonderland, at the distorted landscape that had so thoroughly seduced me with its freedom, its danger, and its delicious, unpredictable rewards.

But then there was that choice, the one lingering in the back of my mind, heavier now with what I knew. I could return to my life in Coral Cove, where things were mundane and ordinary but also safe. Or I could stay here, forever dancing on the knife's edge between liberation and peril.

I took a deep breath, slipping the ring from my finger. The world seemed to fold in on itself, twisting into a kaleidoscope of color and light. I closed my eyes, feeling the air thicken around me, and when I opened them again, I was standing back in Coral Cove, the ocean breeze cool against my skin. It felt jarring and surreal, as though I'd fallen through a trapdoor from one world to the next. I looked down at myself and caught the scent clinging to my clothes—a mixture of sweat, roses, and sex. I needed a shower.

At home, I let the water wash over me, the warmth easing the tension in my muscles. I felt both drained and energized, an odd contradiction, as if my body had been through a war while my mind was still coming to terms with it all. It was hard to shake the feeling of hands on my skin, the echo of the Queen's touch, and that dark thrill of submitting to her power. The memory left me tingling even now, my body still singing from the experience.

By the time I tumbled into bed, I was half-asleep, Wonderland lingering like an imprint on my closed eyelids. I drifted off, uncertain of where I might wake up next.

When morning arrived, the first place I went was back to Lilly Drake. I stepped through the shop's familiar door, its little bell chiming above me, and there was Rainbow behind the counter, as if she'd been expecting me.

"I see you made it back," she said, a knowing smile on her lips.

"Was it real?" I asked, my voice softer than I'd intended. "It felt... I don't know. It felt too intense to be just a dream."

"Oh, it's real all right," she replied, leaning in. "The Fae realm doesn't play by our rules. The pleasures, the dangers—they're all real. When you put that ring on, you're entering their world, and once you're there, it's as much a part of you as you are of it. If you're not certain you want to be there, Alice, and the ring decides to keep you... that will be your reality."

I felt my heart skip, a cold shiver traveling up my spine as her words sank in. The idea that I could've stayed there, perhaps forever, seemed both exhilarating and terrifying.

"Here," I said, sliding the ring across the counter to Rainbow. "I don't think I'm ready to be tempted by it again. Not just yet."

Rainbow nodded, understanding etched into the lines around her eyes. "You're wiser than most. But if you ever change your mind, you know where to find me." She closed her hand over the ring, but I couldn't help but feel the way its absence left my hand oddly bare. I turned to leave, but not without one last glance at the small, unassuming piece of jewelry in her palm.

As I stepped back into the street, I found myself mulling over everything I'd experienced, the rush of Wonderland still thrumming beneath my skin. The choice to leave had been mine, but the taste of that other world lingered, and I knew that someday I might feel its pull again.

For now, though, I walked through Coral Cove with a new appreciation for the quietness, the ordinariness. I saw the world around me differently—its colors, its edges, and its hidden corners. I had glimpsed what was possible, both magical and mundane, and I knew I had the courage to explore either path.

The ring might have been out of sight, but its power, and the thrill of choosing my own fate, remained with me. For the first time, I felt ready to embrace the unknown, no matter which world it might lead me to next.

IF YOU LIKED ALICE AND HER MAD HATTERS, THEN PLEASE check out my other series, Tarot Fantasies.

THE DEVIL'S TEMPTATION
One card, one choice, ultimate temptation.

DOTTIE:

I never believed in fairy tales or silly things like romantic love.

But I drew The Devil card, and his name was Lucian.

When I laid eyes on him, I knew I wouldn't leave The Arcane Room as the same virgin who walked in.

Magic was only real in stories.

Or was it?

SIGN UP FOR MY NEWSLETTER AND GET A FREE BOOK today! https://mailchi.mp/158597581671/jax-wilder

ALSO BY JAX WILDER

Coral Cove Series

Sleighed by Love

Harvesting Love

Dawning Desire

Knead You Now

Love Rewound

Perfect Lover Spell

Haunted by Her

Tarot Fantasies Series

The Devil's Temptations

Strength of the Beast

Hanged Passions

Six of Cups

Death's Embrace

Queen of Pentacles

Seven of Pentacles

Ace of Wands

Three of Swords

Lovers In The Veil

Coastal Cupid Series

HeartBound Souls

Fae Ring Series

Alice and Her Mad Hatters

Stand Alone Titles

Pride and Prejudice and Witches

ADDITIONAL BOOKS BY RAINBOW QUARTZ PUBLISHING

Lorelai Hamilton

Encyclopedia of Divination

Encyclopedia of Cryptids

Encyclopedia of Faeries

Tarot Tales and Magic Spells

Teenage Tarot

Arcane In Verse

The Eclectic Witch's Grimoire

Teenage Witch's Grimoire

Find Your Bliss

Tarot Reflection Journal

Tarot Refection Journal Coloring The Tarot

Dream Journal

Miranda Levi

From A Youth A Fountain Did Flow

The Sea Withdrew

A Tear In Time

Mo(ther) Na(ture)

In Orion's Hands

Jackson Anhalt

From The 911 Files

Isla Watts

A Fairy Bad Day

Surprise! You're a Vampire

Gorgeous, Gorgeous, Gorgons

Mork The Handsome Orc

Adopted By Werewolves

Bite Me If You Can

That's The Spirit!

Rose Dawson's Book Journals

My Time With The Fairies

Enchanted Escapades

Enchanted Escapades

Dewey Decimal Diaries

Siren's Songbook

Pride and Prejudice

Bibliophile's Bounty

Book of Books Journal

Pages & Passages Reading Journal

Bookworm's Companion Reading Journal & Tracker

ABOUT THE AUTHOR

Jax Wilder is a passionate romance author hailing from a charming small town nestled in the picturesque Pacific Northwest. With a heart full of love and an unyielding belief in the power of happily ever afters, Jax weaves enchanting tales of love and connection that leave readers captivated.

Jax's novels are a reflection of her commitment to celebrating the magic of love, and her characters' journeys mirror the warmth and happiness she has found in her own life. Join her on the enchanting journey of love, passion, and enduring connection through her heartfelt romance novels.